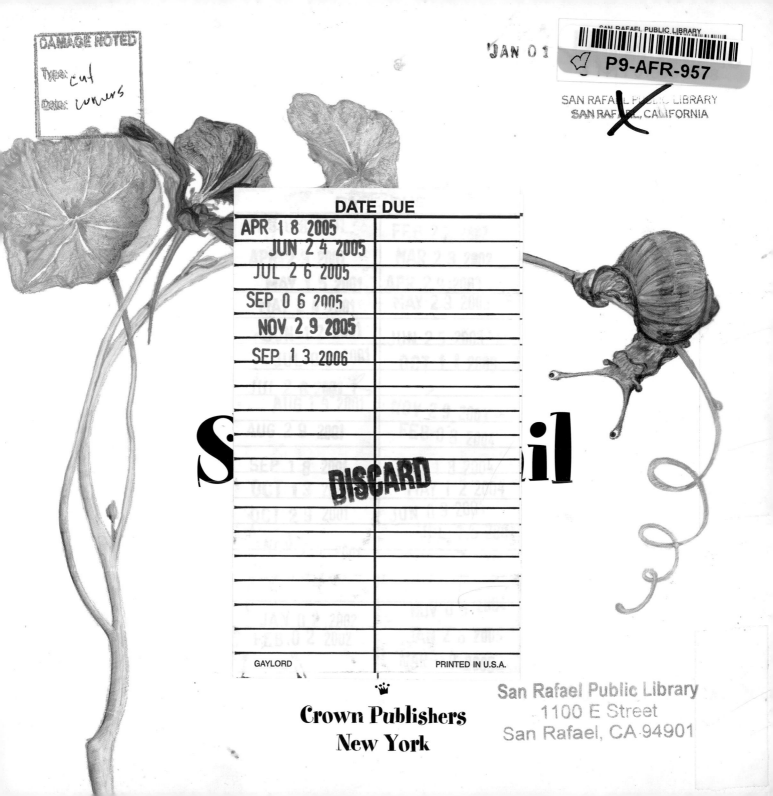

Crown Publishers
New York

Slimy Snail set out on a trail
one bright and sunny morning.

He went up a hill–
it was very steep–

through a tunnel,
very gloomy–

into a forest,
very quiet–

over a bridge,
very high–

down a slope,
very slippery—

up to an arch,
very narrow—

past some flowers,
very pretty–

and into a dark, dark cave.

He curled up in his shell,
very small—

and very soon was
asleep.